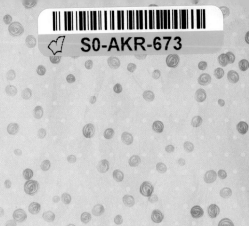

TIME TOGETHER

Me and Grandma

BY MARIA CATHERINE

ILLUSTRATED BY PASCAL CAMPION

PICTURE WINDOW BOOKS

THIS BOOK BELONGS TO:

Family recipe time

Solve the puzzle time

New roots time

Breezy bike time

Summery shade time

Old-fashioned sing-along time

Magical bubble time

Creative paint time

Crazy eights time

Cookie break time

Shopping spree time

Favorite story time

Little smooch time

Sweet sleepover time

Time Together is published by Picture Window Books
A Capstone Imprint
1710 Roe Crest Drive
North Mankato, Minnesota 56003
www.capstonepub.com

Library of Congress Cataloging-in-Publication data
is available on the Library of Congress website.
ISBN: 978-1-4795-5795-0 (paper over board)
ISBN: 978-1-4795-5797-4 (paperback)

Summary:
Time with grandma is always special. From biking to baking,
these small moments are the ones that create big memories
and show the importance of family.

Concepted by:
Kay Fraser and Christianne Jones

Designer:
K. Fraser

Photo Credit:
Shutterstock

Printed in China by Nordica.
0914/CA21401518
092014   008470NORDS15

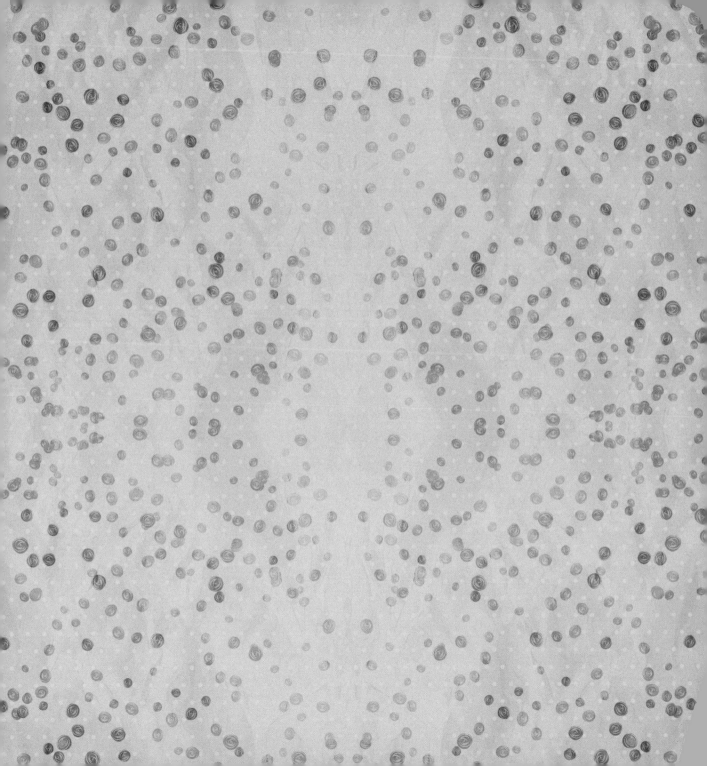

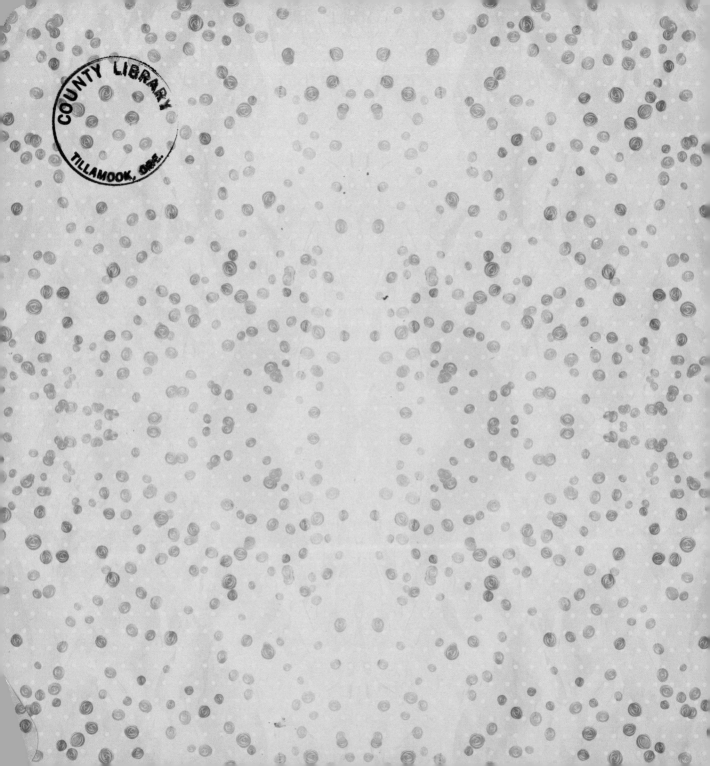